An I Can Read Book®

Old Enough for Magic

story by
Anola Pickett

pictures by
Ned Delaney

HarperTrophy
A Division of HarperCollins*Publishers*

Old Enough for Magic
Text copyright © 1989 by Anola M. Pickett
Illustrations copyright © 1989 by T.N. Delaney, III
Printed in the U.S.A.   All rights reserved.

Library of Congress Cataloging-in-Publication Data
Pickett, Anola.
   Old enough for magic / by Anola Pickett ; pictures by Ned Delaney.
       p.   cm.—(An I can read book)
   Summary: Peter's sister Arlene doesn't think he is old enough to
own a magic set, but when Arlene accidentally turns herself into a
frog, it's Peter who figures out how to get her back.
   ISBN 0-06-024731-2. — ISBN 0-06-024732-0 (lib. bdg.)
   ISBN 0-06-444161-X (pbk.)
   [1. Magic—Fiction.   2. Brothers and sisters—Fiction.]
I. Delaney, Ned, ill.   II. Title.   III. Series.
PZ7.P55253701   1989   88-30320
[E]—dc19   CIP
                                                    AC

First Harper Trophy edition, 1993.

To my brothers Bill, Terry, and Tom
—for all the times I acted like Arlene
A.P.

For Sue, David, and Alex
N.D.

Contents

1

The Birthday Present

It was Peter's birthday.

A big box was on his chair

at breakfast.

"Professor Presto's magic set!"

Peter shouted. "Thank you!"

"We are glad you like it,"

said his father.

"Pooh!" said his sister, Arlene.

"You are too little for magic!"

"I am not," said Peter.

"I am eight years old,

and I am going to my own room

to open my magic set."

"Eight is *not* old enough for magic,"

said Arlene.

Arlene followed him
up the stairs.

"You cannot even win
a game of checkers!"

"You think you are *so* smart

just because you are ten,"

said Peter.

He went into his room

and shut the door.

11

Peter read the words

on his magic set:

PROFESSOR PRESTO'S PACKAGE

OF REAL MAGIC.

Read the red book carefully!

Peter took the red book

out of the box.

He began to read.

A special secret spell

is in the big blue bottle.

Cross your feet

when you say the spell—

or its magic will work on you!

12

Peter took a piece of paper

out of the big blue bottle.

He crossed his feet.

He read the words:

Froggle, fraggle
leaping free.
A fat green
hopper you
will be!

"Peter," called his mother.

"Grandmother is on the phone.

She wants to wish you

a happy birthday."

Peter ran to the telephone.

Arlene tiptoed into Peter's room.

She saw the big blue bottle

and the piece of paper.

"Hmmm," she said,

"what is this?"

Peter came back to his room

just as Arlene said,

"A fat green hopper you will be!"

There was a puff of green smoke.

A chubby green frog

sat in the middle of Peter's rug.

A hair ribbon

was on its head.

"Ribbit! Ribbit!" said the frog.

"Oh, no!" said Peter.

"My sister is a frog!"

2

Old Answers Are Best

"Ribbit! Ribbit! Ribbit!"

said Arlene.

"What should I do now?"

said Peter.

He looked in his magic set.

He opened every box

and shook every bottle.

He read every page of the red book.

Then he saw some words

on the bottom

of the big blue bottle.

Here is how the answer goes—

you will find it under your nose.

"But what does that mean?"

asked Peter.

"Ribbit! Ribbit!" said Arlene.

"I will find someone

to help me," said Peter.

He put Arlene in an old shoe box

and went outside.

Mrs. Potter was working

in her garden.

"Hello, Peter," she said.

"Happy birthday!"

"Hello, Mrs. Potter,"

said Peter.

"You look worried," said Mrs. Potter.

"Is something wrong?"

"Yes," said Peter.

"I have a problem.

What do you do

when *you* have a problem?"

"I tell myself that old answers

are the best answers,"

said Mrs. Potter.

Arlene hopped around

inside the box.

"Ribbit! Ribbit!" she said.

"What do you have in your box?"

asked Mrs. Potter.

"A frog," said Peter.

He opened the lid.

"Goodness!" said Mrs. Potter.

"A frog with a hair ribbon!"

Peter gulped.

"It is a very *special* frog!" he said.

"It must be!" said Mrs. Potter.

"Good luck with your problem!"

Mrs. Potter went back to her garden.

"Good-bye," said Peter.

"What are old answers?"

he wondered.

"What is under my nose?"

"RIB-bit!" croaked Arlene.

She sounded mad.

3

Try the Library

Peter saw his friend Newton

across the street.

"Newton, wait for me!"

Peter shouted.

"Hi, Peter!" said Newton.

"Happy birthday!"

"Thank you," said Peter.

"Can I talk to you?"

"Sure," said Newton.

"What do you do

when you have a problem?"

asked Peter.

"I go to the library
and find a book about it,"
said Newton.
"How do you know
which book to read?"
asked Peter.
"I ask Mr. Simms," said Newton.
He looked at Peter's box.
"Is that a birthday present?"
"Sort of," said Peter.
"Ribbit! Ribbit! Ribbit!"
Arlene was hopping again.

"That sounds like a frog!"
said Newton.

"We can play with it
after my music lesson!"

"Ribbit! Ribbit! Ribbit!
RIBBIT!!!"

Peter felt Arlene bumping

against the lid of the box.

"I am not sure

I will still have it then,"

said Peter.

"I have to go now."

"See you later," said Newton.

Peter hurried to the library.

4

Something You Already Know

Peter stopped

in front of the library.

Ms. Allen came by.

"Hello, Peter!" she said.

"I have a lot of mail for you!"

"Thank you," said Peter.

"Today is my birthday."

"Happy birthday!" said Ms. Allen.

"Ribbit! Ribbit!"

croaked Arlene softly.

"What did you say, Peter?"

asked Ms. Allen.

"Nothing. It was my frog,"

said Peter.

"You don't seem very happy
on your birthday,"
said Ms. Allen.
"Is something wrong?"
"Ms. Allen, what do you do
when you have a problem?"
Peter asked.

Ms. Allen smiled.

"I try to use something
I already know about."

"Thank you," said Peter.

"Maybe that will help me
with my problem."

Peter walked up the steps
to the library.

Would he find a book
about his problem?

What did he already know about?

"Ribbit! Ribbit!" said his sister.

She sounded worried.

5

At the Library

"Hello, Peter," said Mr. Simms.

"Hello, Mr. Simms,"
Peter said.

"Do you have any books
about frogs and magic?"

"We have books about frogs,
and we have books about magic,"
said Mr. Simms.

"Do you want a science book

or a storybook?" asked Mr. Simms.

Peter thought for a minute.

He did not know much about science,

but he knew a *lot* about stories.

He would use something

he already knew about.

"I would like a storybook,"

said Peter.

Mr. Simms looked in the card catalogue.

"Would you like a tale

from long ago?" he asked.

"That would be great!" said Peter.

"Old answers are the best answers!"

"Yes, I suppose so,"

agreed Mr. Simms.

They walked to a tall shelf.

"Here they are," said Mr. Simms.

He handed Peter a thick book

with a beautiful gold cover.

"This book has a story

about a magic frog," said Mr. Simms.

"Ribbit! Ribbit!"

said Arlene.

"Did you say something, Peter?"

asked Mr. Simms.

"No, sir," said Peter.

He hoped Arlene would not croak again.

"Hmmm," said Mr. Simms.

He looked at the box.

"Let me know

if you want any more help."

Peter looked at the list of stories.

There was a story

about a princess and a frog.

Peter read the story.

At the end

the princess kissed the frog.

The frog became a handsome prince.

"OH, NO!" gasped Peter.

"*That* is what the blue bottle said:

The answer is under my nose!"

"Ribbit! RIBBIT! RIBBIT!"

Arlene leaped so high,

she bumped the lid off the box.

She hopped across the library table.

"RIBBIT! RIBBIT! RIBBIT! RIBBIT!"
she croaked loudly.

"Shhhhhhh!" said Peter.

"RRRIB-BIT!"

"Oh, *all right*," said Peter.

"I guess it is the only way.

I hope no one sees me."

He leaned over and

kissed the frog's fat green head.

There was a big puff
of green smoke.

Arlene sat on the table.

"Well, it is about time!" she said.

"I thought I would be
a frog forever!"

"Yuck!" said Peter.

He rubbed his mouth with his hand.

"I am going home."

"Me too!" said Arlene.

6

Old Enough for Magic

Peter and Arlene ran all the way home.

Arlene followed Peter to his room.

Peter walked over to his desk.

He picked up the big blue bottle.

"Put that down!"

screamed Arlene.

"It will trick you!"

"No, it will not," said Peter.

"I read the directions."

"Pooh!" said Arlene.

"You are too little for magic!"

Peter shook his head.

"*I* know how to use the spell.

AND I figured out

how to *break* the spell, too!"

Peter crossed his feet.

"I will show you," he said.

He held up the bottle.

"Wait!" shouted Arlene.

Peter uncrossed his feet.

Arlene looked worried.

"Are you going to turn me

into a frog again?" she asked.

Peter did not say a word.

"Are you?" Arlene yelled,

and stamped her foot.

"Do you think

I am old enough for magic?"

asked Peter.

"You are old enough

to read directions," Arlene said.

Peter crossed his feet again.

He held up the big blue bottle.

"Do you think

I am old enough for *magic*?"

he asked.

Arlene put her hands on her hips.

She glared at Peter.

She looked at the blue bottle.

"Oh, all right!" she said.

"You *are* old enough for magic!"

Arlene stomped out of the room.

Peter smiled

and put his big blue bottle

back into the box.

Arlene never touched

the magic set again.

And Peter almost never lost

another game of checkers.